Introduction to Democracy

Clare Mackie

Contents

Introduction to Democracy

What Is Democracy?

Democracy is a way of organising a government in which everyone gets to vote for the leaders they want. The word "democracy" comes from two Greek words: *demos*, which means "the people", and *kratos*, which means "rule". The idea of democracy was first developed in Greece a long time ago. A country being a democracy meant that instead of having a king or queen, who got the job because they were born into a particular family, the people of the country could make important decisions about who governed them and how they were governed.

The city of Athens in ancient Greece is often called the "birthplace" of democracy.

In a democracy, such as Australia or Aotearoa New Zealand, everyone is treated fairly and has certain rights. Everyone follows the same rules, some of which come from an important international agreement called the Universal Declaration of Human Rights, which declared that everyone in the world should have the same basic rights. People in a democracy can usually say what they think, practise their own religion and protest to make their voices heard when they think something is unfair. However, people must still be mindful not to hurt others or be unfair to any particular group when speaking out. Democracies are good places to live because people are free to do what they want, as long as they are not hurting others or breaking the law.

School kids in the USA make their voices heard by protesting a lack of action on climate change.

Voting and Elections

In a democracy, people choose their leaders by voting in elections. Voting is a group decision, where everyone chooses the **candidate** they each think would be the best leader. In many democracies, including Australia, New Zealand, the USA and Canada, anyone who is 18 years old or older can vote. In some countries, people can vote when they are younger. In Greece, the voting age is 17, and in Austria it is 16.

A candidate who stands for election must be a **citizen** and they must be **eligible** to vote themselves. Candidates usually need to be chosen by a political party, but some people put themselves forward as **independent** candidates. Political parties have different ideas about what are the most important things for governments to do, and the people wanting to be elected represent their party's ideas. Independent candidates have their own ideas.

A young Australian voter makes his choice on election day.

The Secret Ballot

The secret **ballot** system is a type of voting where the voter privately and anonymously marks their choice on a ballot paper. Before this type of voting was introduced, citizens would have to say their vote out loud to the person counting the votes, which meant people around them knew who a voter had voted for.

A secret ballot ensures that the identity of the voter is protected. This is important because it stops voters from being threatened or **intimidated** by people who might want to influence an election.

This style of ballot was first introduced in Tasmania, Australia, in 1856, and so this method of voting is also called the "Australian Ballot". After it was introduced in Australia, the idea spread to Europe and the USA. In 1870, New Zealand also adopted this method.

An Australian voter puts their anonymous ballot paper into a ballot box after making their choice.

Preferential Voting

In the system called preferential voting, voters nominate their first, second and following choices, or "preferences", for candidates for a single position. If no candidate achieves a majority (more than 50 per cent) of first-place votes, the votes for the least popular candidate are recounted according to the second choice of each voter. If, after this first recount, no candidate receives a majority, then the next least popular candidate's votes are recounted. This process continues until one candidate is the clear winner.

In a preferential voting system, there are sometimes a large number of candidates, so ballot papers can be very large.

What Happens on Election Day?

When voting closes, workers sort the votes to see how many each party got.

Throughout election night, updates are provided as each polling station finishes counting, and the country waits to find out which party will be the new government.

Voting Around the World

Around the world, different countries have different systems for voting. In some countries, like Chile and Hungary, individuals are automatically registered to vote when they turn 18. In Australia, citizens have to register themselves. People who live in New Zealand, Tonga or the United Kingdom can be fined for not registering to vote.

Some countries allow their citizens to send their vote in the mail. Postal votes are most widely used in Europe and North America. Most countries rely on ballot papers, but some countries, like India and the USA, also use electronic voting machines. Switzerland allows its citizens to vote online. In Gambia, voting is done by placing marbles into drums, due to many citizens not having learnt to read and write.

A woman votes by mail.

A woman uses an electronic voting machine in India.

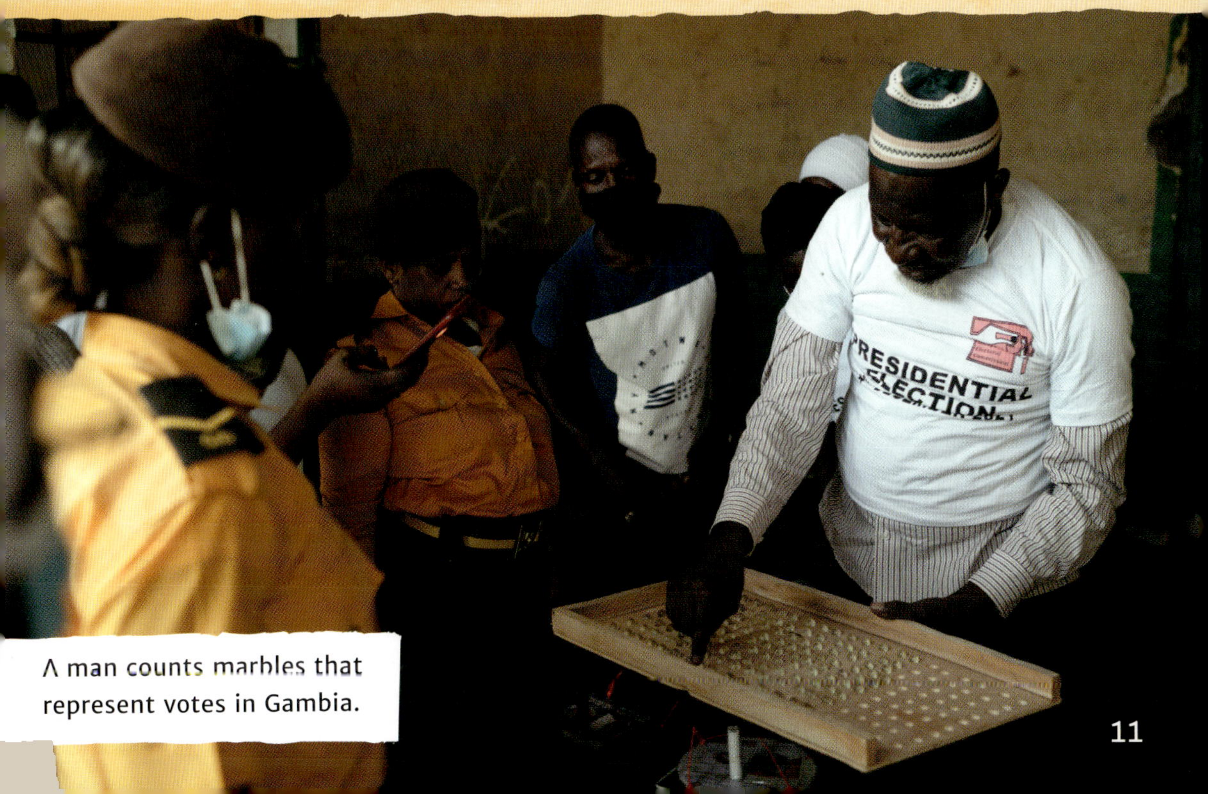

A man counts marbles that represent votes in Gambia.

During the height of the Covid-19 pandemic, people wore masks and avoided crowded indoor places.

Before the Covid-19 pandemic, only about a quarter of countries used postal voting for their elections. But many countries expanded their postal voting options as a result of the pandemic, because of concerns about voter health and safety in crowded polling stations.

In some countries, it is compulsory to vote. Compulsory voting means that every eligible citizen is legally required to attend a voting booth on election day and cast their vote. Unless someone has a valid excuse, not voting can result in a fine. Compulsory voting is used in some countries, like Australia, to make sure everyone has a say in who is elected to government. Many other countries, including New Zealand, the USA and Canada, do not have compulsory voting.

The Right to Vote

A "right" is something that a person is allowed to *have* or *do* that is protected by law or by a set of rules. Rights are things that everyone should *have* access to, like housing, healthcare, **sanitation** and education. Rights are also things that people are free to *do* without anyone, including the government, interfering, such as the right to practise a religion, or to express opinions, or to protest against something.

Many of the rights enjoyed by citizens in democracies are based on the basic rights and freedoms set out in the Universal Declaration of Human Rights.

People who grow up in a democracy have the right to an education.

Voting is an important right. However, not all countries allow all of their people to vote. India is a democracy, but a law there makes it harder for many people who practise the Islamic religion to become citizens. People affected by this law cannot vote in elections.

In India, people who practise the Islamic religion and people who practise the Hindu religion live side by side, but they do not have all the same rights.

Saudi Arabia is a monarchy, meaning its government is led by a king, but there are some elections for local governments. Up until 2015, women were not permitted to vote in any elections in Saudi Arabia. Even today, many women do not vote because they never registered to do so.

While some people have had the right to vote in Australia and New Zealand since the 1800s, many people were excluded. Men who owned or leased property of a certain value could vote. However, First Nations people and women in Australia and New Zealand had to fight for their right to vote. The rules have changed over the last 150 years to create a fairer system.

Sydney, Australia, in 1890

First Nations Peoples

While many men were given the right to vote in the mid-1800s in Australia and New Zealand, this right did not generally extend to First Nations men.

In Australia, First Nations men who owned property could vote in some state elections before 1901, when the country **federated**. After federation, First Nations men were still allowed to vote in some states, but there were many unfair rules that made it difficult. A **racist** law in 1902 excluded First Nations men from voting in **federal elections**. This law wasn't changed until 1962, when all First Nations people were finally allowed to vote in federal elections.

First Nations men and women in Australia were prevented from voting in most elections until 1962.

First Nations Māori men in New Zealand gained the right to vote in 1867, but only in four special **electorates** for Māori people. Since 1975, Māori people can choose to vote in either the Māori electorates or the general electorates.

Women

For much of history, across the world, women have not had the same rights as men, even in democracies. In the late 1800s, more and more women began fighting for their rights, including the right to earn their own money, to own their own property and to vote.

In 1893, New Zealand became the first country in the world in which women won the right to vote in **national** elections. In 1894, South Australia became the first state in Australia in which women had the right to vote, and by 1902, Australian women could vote in federal elections. First Nations women and men were excluded from this right, however.

Gaining the right to vote was a significant change for women, who did not have many rights at the time compared to today. When a woman got married, her husband would control all of her money and property. Women winning the right to vote was an important sign that society was changing. The countries that gave women the vote were seen to be more **progressive**.

Women march to demand the right to vote in New York, USA, in 1915.

What Happens After an Election

After an election, the amount of change that occurs depends on which party won the most votes. If the party that is already in power wins, then things continue as before. But if a different party wins, there is a process for the orderly transfer of power and responsibility to the new **representatives**. This process ensures that power transfers peacefully, and that the newly elected representatives can do their jobs well.

First, the incoming leader is **sworn in**. After that, the leader decides which members of their party will take on the different jobs in the government. The exiting party members who used to do these jobs sometimes prepare information for them, to help them understand the key projects and issues that were being worked on.

A member of the government gives a speech in Parliament House, Australia.

The Responsibilities of a Leader

The most important job in a government is that of the leader. In some democracies, such as Australia and New Zealand, the leader is called the prime minister, and in others, such as the USA, the leader is called the president. The difference between the two is that a prime minister is chosen by the elected members of the political party that won the election, whereas a president is elected directly by the citizens through a voting system.

The prime minister or president leads the entire country. In some democracies, including Australia and the USA, there are also state leaders. These are called premiers in Australia and governors in the USA.

Researchers have studied the qualities that people look for in their political candidates. They found that honesty and trustworthiness were the most valued **traits**.

Other important qualities included leadership abilities, having a positive impact and being able to listen and change with a situation.

Former New Zealand Prime Minister Jacinda Ardern gives a speech.

The leader of the government carries out different tasks depending on the country's system of government. Some common responsibilities of government leaders include:

- selecting and managing the other members of their government
- leading the government in following through on what they promised to the citizens during their election campaign
- making key decisions about the issues that face their government, including the management of the economy
- communicating clearly to citizens about what the government is doing
- representing their state or country in national or international meetings and discussions
- responding to national emergencies, such as natural disasters.

Parliament House in Australia

the Beehive parliament building in New Zealand

the Capitol Building in the USA

Often, citizens also vote for local government candidates in elections. The local government leader is often called the mayor. Local governments are responsible for local issues, such as building houses and roads, disposing of rubbish and providing parks for local communities.

People living in democracies enjoy many rights and freedoms. Many people have fought hard to ensure that the rules and laws of democracies are fair and treat everyone equally. It is important to understand the different political parties, how the government works, and the voting process, so that the hard work of all those who have come before is respected.

People in a democracy can live more freely, knowing that their rights are protected.

A Democracy Timeline

1215, Great Britain

A document called the **Magna Carta** is signed by King John that states that there are limits on a king's power. Before this, a king had full control over citizens.

1840, New Zealand

The **Treaty of Waitangi** is an agreement between the British government and Māori chiefs in New Zealand. It sets out important ideas about working together, looking after each other and everyone having a say.

1689, Great Britain

The **Bill of Rights** is passed. This law states that everyone in Great Britain has certain rights, including the right to a fair trial so everyone can prove their innocence or guilt, and freedom of speech so people can say what they want without getting into trouble.

1200 1300 1400 1500

1894, Australia

The **Constitutional Amendment (Adult Suffrage) Act** is passed in South Australia, allowing most women to vote in state elections and run for state office.

1863, USA

The **Emancipation Proclamation** is made by President Abraham Lincoln during the American Civil War, which states that all enslaved people in the USA must be free.

1867, New Zealand

The **Māori Representation Act** creates four electorates just for Māori men to vote for their own members of parliament.

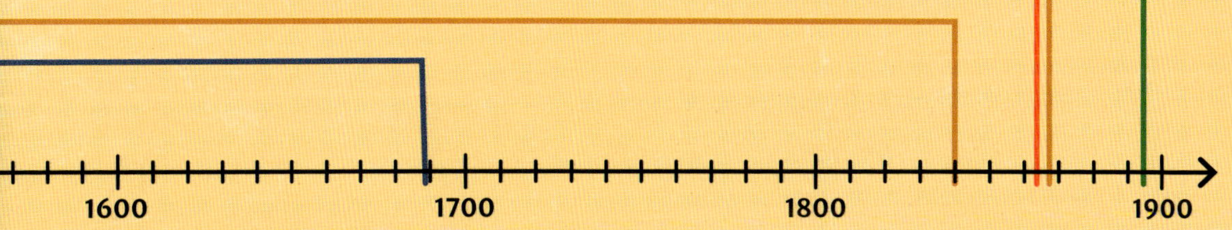

1902, Australia

The **Commonwealth Franchise Act** is passed, allowing most women to vote in national elections and run for federal office.

1948

The **Universal Declaration of Human Rights** sets out the basic rights and freedoms that all human beings around the world are entitled to, regardless of race, gender, religion or other characteristics.

1962, Australia

The **Commonwealth Electoral Act** is passed, allowing all First Nations people to vote in federal elections.

1900 1910 1920 1930 1940 1950

1964, USA

The Civil Rights Act is passed, stating that nobody can be treated unfairly because of their skin colour, beliefs, gender, where they come from or their religion.

1967, Australia

In the 1967 Referendum, a large majority of people vote "Yes" to the question of whether Australia's **Constitution** should be changed so that First Nations Australians are counted in the **census** and treated the same as other Australians.

2017, Australia

In a **postal survey**, a majority of people voted that they agreed that two people of the same gender should have the right to marry; after this, a law was passed making this change. Many other countries had already passed this law, including Canada in 2005 and New Zealand in 2013.

1960 1970 1980 1990 2000 2010 2020

My School Election

Yesterday was a really exciting day, because we had the vote for school captain. I had been hoping to take on this role since I first came to my school.

Before the vote, all of the candidates had to present a speech at assembly in front of the whole school. There were a few good candidates for people to choose from, and some of my classmates made some impressive promises to get votes. Like Jo, who declared that she would organise a different type of tag game every day. While this was a pretty good idea, I knew that it wouldn't appeal to everyone. Some people might even choose not to vote for her based on her promise.

When it was my turn, my heart was beating so hard, I thought it might jump right out of my chest. But I took a deep breath and smiled, trying not to show anyone I was nervous. I had practised my speech at home, so by the time I walked up to the stage I was able to speak confidently and look at the audience.

I told the school that I felt proud to be speaking to them because I wanted people to know I cared about the school. Next, I shared my idea, which was that everyone could make a suggestion about the sort of activities they wanted to see happen at lunchtime. I promised I would do my best to organise as many activities as I could between now and the end of the year. Lots of kids smiled at me when I said that, and nodded their heads, which made me feel even more confident.

I finished my speech by telling the students that voting for me would give them freedom of choice. I thought it was important to make a connection to what we had been learning in our classroom about rights. We are so lucky to have the right to follow our chosen religion or protest about things we are unhappy about. And even though the kids in younger year levels hadn't been learning about rights in class and may not all have understood democracy, I was sure they would understand that protecting free choice was a good thing.

After the speeches finished, everyone went back to their classrooms to vote. The teacher handed each student in my class a piece of paper with all the names of the students who had put themselves forward to be considered for school captain. We had to number our top three choices, putting a number 1 next to our first preference, a 2 next to our second preference and a 3 next to our third preference.

When everyone had made their decision, my teacher collected the papers. He explained that he would count up the votes during lunchtime, and email through the totals to the principal's office. Once all the classes in the school had submitted their points, the school captain would be announced at tomorrow's assembly.

Overall, putting my name forward to be considered for school captain yesterday was a very valuable experience. I was really nervous presenting my speech, but because I had practised so many times, I was able to deliver my message clearly and confidently. And I discovered that I actually enjoyed speaking to everyone and connecting with my audience.

This is probably a good thing, because I found out at assembly today that I was chosen to be school captain, so I will be making a lot of speeches this year!

Glossary

ballot (*noun*)	the system of voting by writing down your choice
candidate (*noun*)	a person who wants to be elected to a position in a government
census (*noun*)	a survey taken by a government to gather information about the population
citizen (*noun*)	a person who belongs to a country and has the same rights as everybody else there
constitution (*noun*)	the basic laws and principles of a country, usually recorded in a document
electorates (*noun*)	areas represented by one member of parliament (MP)
eligible (*adjective*)	having the right to do something
federal elections (*noun*)	elections to choose the leaders of a whole country
federated (*verb*)	joined together to become one country with a central government
independent (*adjective*)	not belonging to a political party
intimidated (*verb*)	pressured or made to feel unsafe
national (*adjective*)	related to an entire country, rather than a state or territory
polling stations (*noun*)	buildings where people go to vote in elections

postal survey (*noun*) questionnaires mailed out to people to get their opinion about an issue

progressive (*adjective*) in favour of change and new ideas

racist (*adjective*) unfair towards people because of their race

registered (*verb*) recorded in an official list

representatives (*noun*) people elected to speak and act for the people of an area

sanitation (*noun*) a system to keep places clean and safe from disease

sworn in (*verb*) given a role at an official ceremony at which the person swears, or promises, to do their duties well

traits (*noun*) qualities or characteristics

Index